Louella Mae,
She's Run Away!

Karen Beaumont Alarcón

Illustrations by Rosanne Litzinger

Henry Holt and Company • New York

Louella Mae,
she's run away!

Look in the cornfields!
Look in the hay!
Where, oh where, is Louella Mae?

Fetch the ol' hound dog!
Fetch all your kin!
Louella Mae's run away again!

She's not in the cornfields!
She's not in the hay!
Where, oh where, is Louella Mae?

Round up the horses!
Hitch up the team!
Hop in the buckboard
and look by the . . .

...*stream.*

Has *anyone* seen her?
Now where could she be?
Go look in the
hollowed-out trunk of that...

...tree.

Set down your washboards,
your needles, and yarn!
And see if she's hiding
out there in the . . .

...barn.

She's not by the stream,
nor the barn, nor the tree.
Where, oh where, could Louella Mae be?

In the woods! There's a shadow!
Go look over there
'fore she gets swallered up
by a big ol' black . . .

...bear.

Did somebody snatch her?
A banshee or witch?
Or did she get caught
in the vines by the...

Run tell the neighbors
and y'all give a yell
'fore she wanders off yonder
and falls in the...

...well.

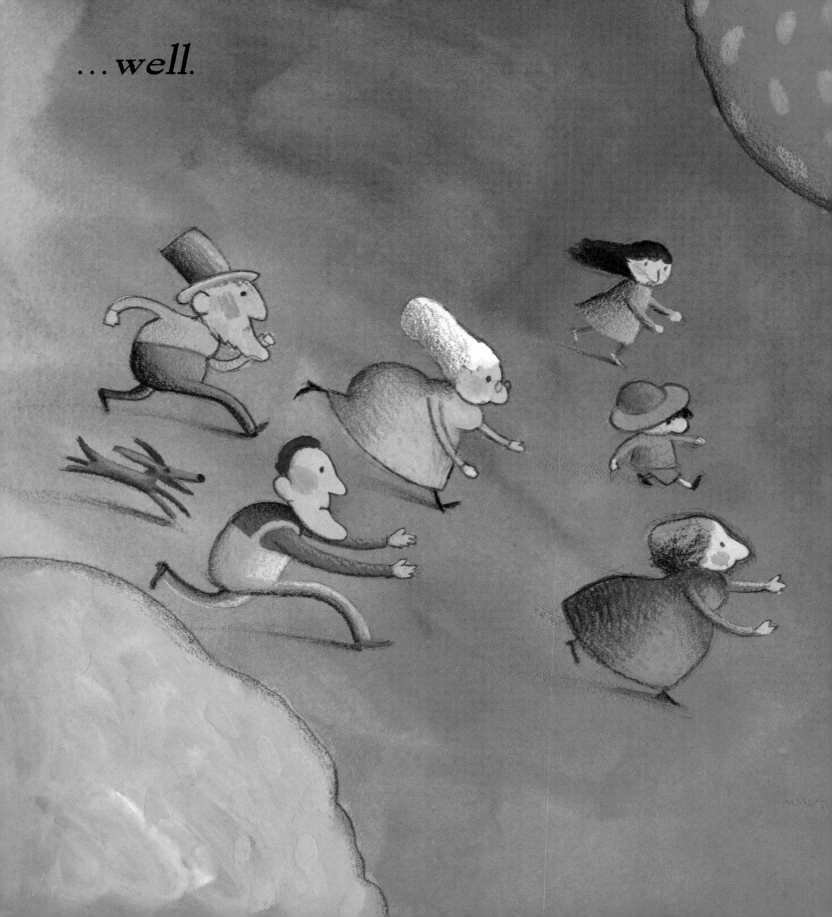

Has anyone seen her?
Does anyone know?
Where, oh where, did Louella Mae go?

Look! Is that her?
Is she lost on the ridge?

Or could she be stuck
in the muck 'neath the...

...bridge?

We've looked! We can't find her,
not here and not there.

Is she this way? Or that way?
Or which way? Or where?

Nightfall's a-coming!
Oh mercy, I swan!
It looks like Louella Mae
really is gone.

Hey, Ma! Go tell Pa!
Uncle Henry and Chub!
We found her! She's sleeping
inside in the...

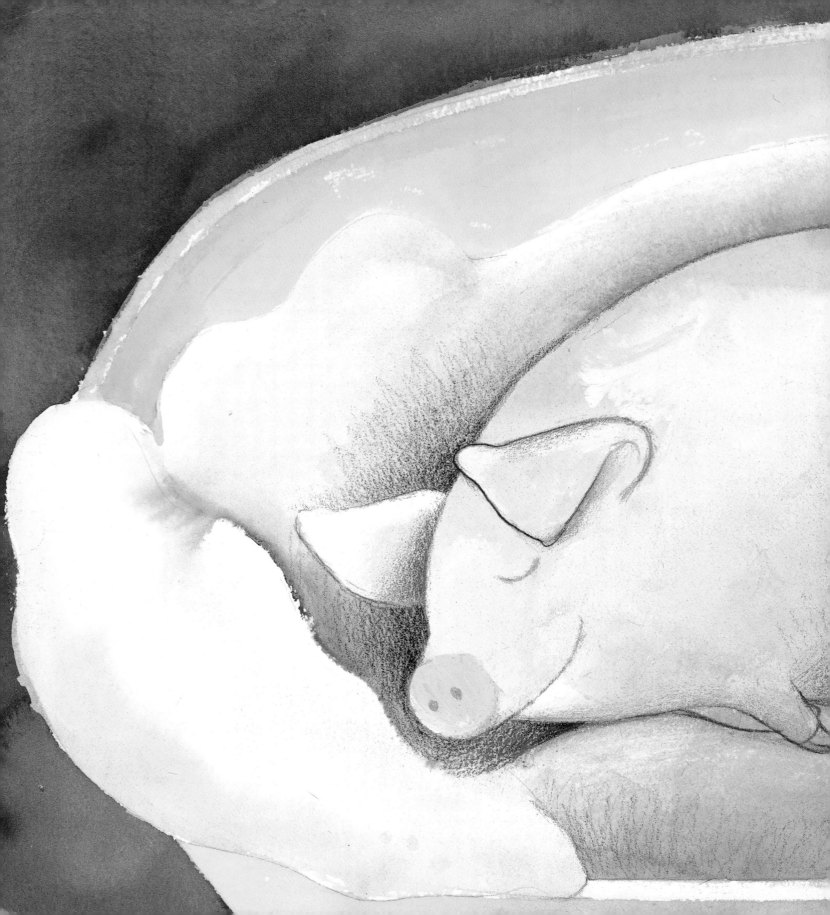

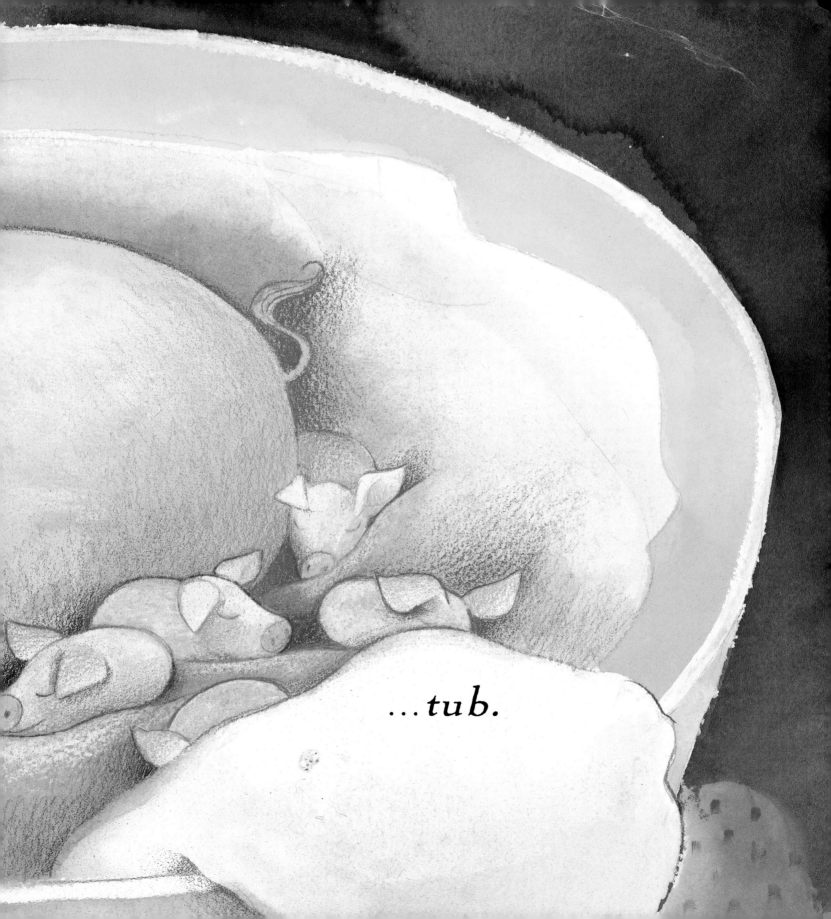

...*tub.*

For my mom and dad with love

—K. A.

For Louella Mae's audience with best wishes

—R. L.

In memory of the *real* Louella Mae Cherry Allgood, my friend and senior-adult exercise student, who was born in Hollywood, Arkansas, in 1894. On her ninety-seventh birthday she told me, "Yep, when I got married and moved to Oklahoma, my friends in Arkansas used to say, 'Louella Mae, she run away!'" Her words and spirit inspired this book.

—K. A.

Henry Holt and Company, LLC, *Publishers since 1866*
175 Fifth Avenue, New York, New York 10010 [www.HenryHoltKids.com]

Henry Holt ® is a registered trademark of Henry Holt and Company, LLC.
Text copyright © 1997 by Karen Beaumont Alarcón. Illustrations copyright © 1997 by Rosanne Litzinger
All rights reserved.
Distributed in Canada by H. B. Fenn and Company Ltd.

Library of Congress Cataloging-in-Publication Data
Alarcón, Karen Beaumont. Louella Mae, she's run away! / Karen Beaumont Alarcón ; illustrations by Rosanne Litzinger.
Summary: A growing crowd searches all around for the missing Louella Mae.
[1. Lost and found possessions—Fiction. 2. Pigs—Fiction. 3. Stories in rhyme.]
I. Litzinger, Rosanne, ill. II. Title.
PZ8.3.A329Lo 1996 [E]—dc20 96-12319

ISBN 978-0-8050-3532-2 (hardcover)
7 9 10 8 6
ISBN 978-0-8050-6830-6 (paperback)
7 9 10 8 6

First published in hardcover in 1997 by Henry Holt and Company.
First paperback edition, 2002

Designed by Martha Rago
The artist used watercolor with colored pencils and black-ink line
on Arches fine watercolor paper to create the illustrations for this book.

Printed in March 2010 in China by South China Printing Company Ltd.,
Dongguan City, Guangdong Province, on acid-free paper. ∞